FINN'S
Marching Band

A Story of Counting, Colors, and Playing Together

Written and Illustrated by
Rachelle Evensen

Ambassador
Children's Books
New York/Mahwah, NJ

For my Lord, my Savior, my Song—
Only by following Your rhythm do I keep the beat.

For Derek, my noble prince—
Thank you for all the PBJs you made, the rocket rides you gave, and the
tucking in you did to make this book a reality. I love you so very much!

Text and art copyright © 2009 Rachelle Evensen

Library of Congress Cataloging-in-Publication Data

Evensen, Rachelle.
  Finn's marching band / written and illustrated by Rachelle Evensen.
     p. cm.
  Summary: Much to his surprise, a drum-playing little duck becomes the
leader of a marching band as progressively larger groups of farm animals
join him in merry music-making. Includes Bible verses.
  ISBN 978-0-8091-6749-4 (alk. paper)
  [1. Ducks--Fiction. 2. Domestic animals--Fiction. 3. Music--Fiction. 4.
Marching bands--Fiction. 5. Christian life--Fiction. 6. Counting.] I.
Title.
  PZ7.E9146Fi 2010
  [E]--dc22
                          2009022436

Published by Ambassador Books
An imprint of Paulist Press
997 Macarthur Boulevard
Mahwah, New Jersey 07430

www.ambassadorbooks.com

Printed and bound in China

Whatever you do, work at it with all your heart.

— Colossians 3:23

One yellow duck named Finn was playing
his drum and marching around the barn.
He was stepping in time to the dup-a-dup-dup
of his drumbeats.

Two orange kittens wanted to march.
They brought their kazoos and fell in step behind Finn.
"Why are you following me?" asked Finn.
"We want to be in your marching band," said the kittens.
"But I'm just a little yellow duck playing a drum,"
said Finn. "I can't lead a marching band."

But the kittens played, "Zoop, zoop, zoop."
And so Finn played, "Dup-a-dup-dup."

3

One yellow duck named Finn and
two orange kittens were marching around the barn.
Three pink piglets wanted to march.
They fetched their tubas and fell in step behind Finn.

"We want to be in your marching band," said the piglets.
"But I'm just a little yellow duck playing a drum," said Finn.
"I can't lead a marching band."
All the same, the piglets played, "Oompah, oompah, oompah."
And Finn played, "Dup-a-dup-dup."

One yellow duck named Finn,
two orange kittens, and
three pink piglets were marching around the barn.
Four black calves wanted to march.
They fetched their cow bells and fell in step behind Finn.

"We want to be in your marching band," said the calves.
"But I'm just a little yellow duck playing a drum," said Finn.
"I can't lead a marching band."
Nevertheless, the calves played, "Clankity, clank, clank."
And Finn played, "Dup-a-dup-dup."

5

One yellow duck named Finn,

two orange kittens,

three pink piglets, and

four black calves were marching around the barn.

Five gray goats wanted to march.

They fetched their trumpets and fell

in step behind Finn.

"We want to be in your marching band," said the goats.
"But I'm just a little yellow duck playing a drum," said Finn.
"I can't lead a marching band."
Even so, the goats played,
"Toot, toot-a-loo, toot-a-loo."
And Finn played, "Dup-a-dup-dup."

One yellow duck named Finn,

two orange kittens,

three pink piglets,

four black calves,

and five gray goats were marching around the barn.

Six brown foals wanted to march.

They fetched their tambourines and fell in step behind Finn.

"We want to be in your marching band," said the foals.
"But I'm just a little yellow duck playing a drum," said Finn.
"I can't lead a marching band."
But the foals played, "Chink, chink, jingle."
And Finn played, "Dup-a-dup-dup."

One yellow duck named Finn,
two orange kittens,
three pink piglets,
four black calves,
five gray goats,
and six brown foals were marching around the barn.
Seven green frogs wanted to march.
They fetched their piccolos and fell in step behind Finn.

"We want to be in your marching band,"
said the frogs.
"But I'm just a little yellow duck
playing a drum," said Finn.
"I can't lead a marching band."

Nonetheless, the frogs played,
"Pickle, pickle, piccolo."
And Finn played, "Dup-a-dup-dup."

8

One yellow duck named Finn,
two orange kittens,
three pink piglets,
four black calves,
five gray goats,
six brown foals,
and seven green frogs were marching around the barn.
Eight red hens wanted to march.
They fetched their saxophones and fell in step behind Finn.

"We want to be in your marching band,"
said the hens.
"But I'm just a little yellow duck
playing a drum," said Finn.
"I can't lead a marching band."
Still, the hens played,
"Swoop, swing, swing."
And Finn played,
"Dup-a-dup-dup."

One yellow duck named Finn,
two orange kittens,
three pink piglets,
four black calves,
five gray goats,
six brown foals,
seven green frogs,
and eight red hens were marching around the barn.
Nine white lambs wanted to march.
They fetched their cymbals and fell in step behind Finn.

"We want to be in your marching band," said the lambs.

"But I'm just a little yellow duck playing a drum," said Finn. "I can't lead a marching band."

But the lambs played, "Clash, smash, clash."

And Finn played, "Dup-a-dup-dup."

10

One yellow duck named Finn,
two orange kittens,
three pink piglets,
four black calves,
five gray goats,
six brown foals,

seven green frogs,

eight red hens, and

nine white lambs were marching around the barn.

Ten golden honeybees wanted to march,

so they fell in step behind Finn.

"We want to be in your marching band,"
said the honeybees.
"But how can you be in a marching band?"
asked Finn. "I'm just a little yellow duck playing
a drum, and even I can see that you can't march."

The bees replied, "Sure we can march. We march on the air!"
"But where are your instruments?" asked Finn.
"Well," said the honeybees, "you are a little yellow duck playing
a drum, just as God made you—and you can lead a marching
band. We are honeybees, just as God made us. We may not have
instruments, but we can play our buzz!"

"Okey dokey," said Finn, with a shrug. "Welcome to my marching band!"

"Ready, Finn's Marching Band?
Let's make some joyful noise!
And a one, and a two,
and a one-two-three-four!"

10 So ten golden honeybees sang, "Buzzy, buzz, buzz."

9 Nine white lambs played, "Clash, smash, clash."

8 Eight red hens played, "Swoop, swing, swing,"

7 Seven green frogs played, "Pickle, pickle, piccolo."

6 Six brown foals played, "Chink, chink, jingle."

5 Five gray goats played, "Toot, toot-a-loo, toot-a-loo."

4 Four black calves played, "Clankity, clank, clank."

3 Three pink piglets played, "Oompah, oompah, oompah."

2 Two orange kittens played, "Zoop, zoop, zoop."

1 And one yellow duck named Finn played, "Dup-a-dup-dup."

Make a joyful noise to the LORD, all the earth.
Worship the LORD with gladness;
come into his presence with singing.

— Psalm 100:1–2